This annual belongs to

....

....

Write your name here

EGMONT
We bring stories to life

First published in Great Britain in 2015 by Egmont UK Limited,
The Yellow Building, 1 Nicholas Road, London, W11 4AN

Written by Catherine Such.
Designed by Jeannette O'Toole.

ISBN 978 1 4052 7794 5
60297/1
Printed in Italy

Annual 2016

The DOC is in

Contents

Say Hello

Let's meet Doc McStuffins and her friends.

Doc

Doc McStuffins is a kind and caring doctor who looks after poorly stuffed animals and toys. She has a magic stethoscope that brings them to life.

Stuffy

Stuffy is a toy dragon with a big roar. He's very brave, but terribly clumsy and is always bumping into things!

Lambie

Loveable Lambie is Doc's best friend. Her favourite thing in the world is giving cuddles – she's always on hand when a patient needs a hug.

Hallie

Helpful Hallie is a big hippo with a big heart. She's a nurse at Doc's clinic and makes sure everywhere is clean and tidy.

Chilly

Snowman Chilly worries about everything, but he always feels better after a check-up from Doc.

Colour the flower next to your favourite character.

Find the Friends

Read these questions then point to the right friend.

1 Who has wings?

2 Who is wearing a scarf?

3 Who is carrying a bag?

4 Who is wearing a pink bow?

5 Who is dressed in stripes?

Answers on page 68.

Let's Explore!

This is Doc's surgery, isn't it cool? There are lots of interesting things in here like Doc's tools, her toys and her crayons.

Can you spot them all?

Doc's checklist

Tick each item as you find it.

Answers on page 68.

One Note Wonder

1 Donny and Alma are singing a song in the garden. Donny is playing his toy drums. Alma is playing her toy xylophone.

2 Doc thinks they sound great! She joins in the song on the kazoo. This band is really rocking!

3 "Wait, my xylophone sounds funny," says Alma. "One of the keys doesn't make the right noise, listen."

'Thud! Thud!' goes the key. "That's strange, shall I take a look at it for you, Alma?" asks Doc.

4

Doc takes the xylophone to her surgery and magics all the toys to life. "This musical patient needs our help," she says.

5

"Hello, I'm Xyla," says the xylophone. "I love music too," shouts Stuffy. "Check this out, BOOM, ch-ka, BOOM!"

6

"OK, Xyla, I'm going to use my stethoscope to hear how you sound," says Doc. "Hmm, I think I can see where the problem is."

"Here's your magnifying glass, Doc," says Stuffy. "Thanks, Stuffy ... aha! I have a diagnosis!" cries Doc.

7

"What's the problem?" asks Hallie. "Xyla has Loose Key Syndrome," says Doc. "This screw is undone so the key is loose."

8

"So it is," says Stuffy as he prods Xyla's key. Uh-oh, Stuffy has made the key fly through the air! It's heading for the sink!

9

The key falls down the plughole. "It's lost!" cries Xyla. "Don't worry," says Doc. "Let's look in my spare parts box."

"Look!" says Xyla. "There's a key hidden in the box! It's like the one I lost!"
"It looks good but will it fit?" asks Hallie.

11

"I need my special screwdriver," says Doc. It takes a moment ... TING! Doc hits the key and it sounds perfect.

12 "Thanks, Doc!" cries Xyla, happily. "I was worried I'd never play again. You rock!"
"Now let's rock to the music!" laughs Doc, as the toys start to dance around the surgery.

the end

Bath Time

Bath Buddies

Doc's friends love their bath time toys, but who owns each one?

 1

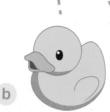 2

 3

a

b

c

Time for the Tub

Can you match each object up to its shadow?

1

2

3

4

a

b

c

d

16

Answers on page 68.

Daring Differences

Can you spot five differences between these two pictures of the brave knight?

Tick them as you find them.

Did you find them all?

Answers on page 68.

Huge Hug

Doc is giving Lambie a big cuddle to help her feel better.

Use your brightest crayons to colour them in.

Pet Vet

Doc is taking care of her furry friends, but she's lost her bag. Can you lead her through the maze to find it?

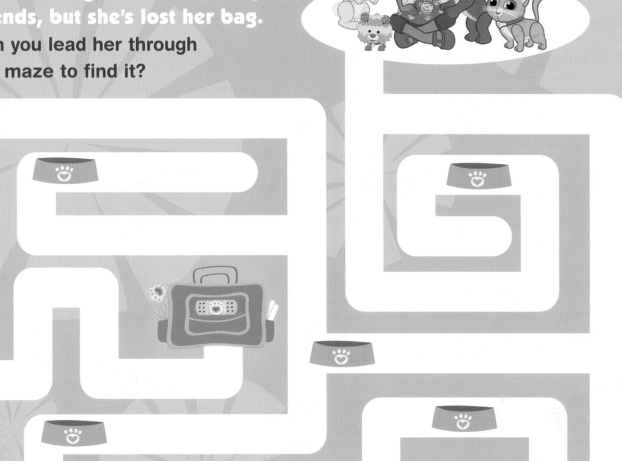

How many dog bowls can you count in the maze? Trace over the correct number.

5 or 6

Answers on page 68.

Colour Fun

Grab your favourite pens or crayons to complete these exciting colour activities.

Tracing Time

Trace over the letters then colour these objects in the correct colours.

red

green

Doctor's Kit

What colour is Doc's bag?
Put a tick in the correct box.

 orange

 pink

Daring Dragon

Use a blue pen or crayon to colour this picture of Stuffy.

Riding Around

Doc is taking her friends for a ride. Can you point to three purple things in this happy picture?

Answers on page 68.

21

Cuddle Time

Doc has made her monkey friends feel better again.
Which jigsaw piece finishes this happy picture?

Circle the missing piece.

a

b

c

Answers on page 68.

Doc's Doodles

Doc likes to draw pictures of the toys she's helped in her Big Book of Boo-Boos.

Can you draw a picture of your favourite toy below?

Starry, Starry Night

Read this story and when you see a picture, shout the word out loud!

Doc

telescope

Henry

stars

stethoscope

It is a clear evening and is in the garden.

Her friend has brought round his new

 so they can look at the .

 opens the box and puts the

together but something isn't right. "Everything

looks blurry," sighs.

"I'm good at fixing toys, perhaps I can fix your

telescope," says . "That would be great!"

cheers .

Doc takes the to her surgery.
With a touch of her magic , the
comes to life.

"Hi, Doc, I'm Aurora," says the . Oops,
Aurora doesn't seem to notice that she's bumping
into everything!

"Aurora, I think we need to give your eyesight a
check-up," says 🧑🏽‍⚕️ . "It's time for an eye test."

🧑🏽‍⚕️ points to a giraffe picture on her eye test
screen. "What's that?" she asks. "It's a banana,"
says Aurora. Oh dear!

"It's not a banana but I do have a diagnosis," says
🧑🏽‍⚕️ . "You have Blurrystaritis." Stuffy wants to
know what that is.

"Well, to us 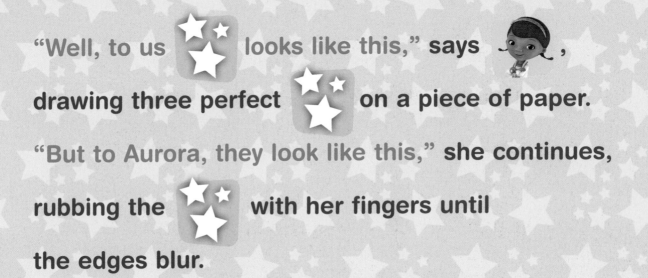 looks like this," says ,
drawing three perfect on a piece of paper.
"But to Aurora, they look like this," she continues,
rubbing the with her fingers until
the edges blur.

"Will I ever be able to see clearly?" Aurora asks.
"Sure," answers . "There are lots of things a
doctor can do to help your eyes."

"That's why I wear glasses," says Hallie. "They
help me to see clearly. Without them everything
looks blurry."

"Hmmm, maybe there's something Aurora needs to
help her see more clearly," says . She
picks up the box that Aurora was stored in. "That's
it!" cries. "You're missing your eye piece."

26

"Maybe dropped it when he was putting the together," suggests Stuffy. "Let's go back to the garden and have a look," says .

 and her friends explore the garden. "Here it is!" cries . She picks up the eye piece and fits it onto Aurora. "Is that better?" asks. "Yes, I can see again!" cries Aurora. "Thank you." "No problem," says . "Now, let's go and look at some ."

 picks up Aurora and the friends take it in turns to look through the at the twinkling . "What an amazing sight," sighs and everyone else agrees.

Did you like our story?

27

The Doc is In!

Doc's surgery is open! Lend a hand by solving these puzzles.

Counting Fun

How many plasters can you count?

Write your answer in the box. ☐ **plasters**

Little Lambie

Draw a circle around the smallest picture of Lambie.

28

Time to Play!

Doc has brought a toy to cheer her patients up. Trace over the dotted lines to find out what it is.

What game do you think Doc's friends will play with the toy?

[ ] Hide and Seek   [ ] Catch   [ ] Pass the Parcel

29

Answers on page 68.

The Letter d

Doc's name begins with the letter d. Can you find four other things that start with the letter d? Draw a circle around each one.

Let's practise! Trace over the letter d starting at the star.

dddd

Answers on page 68.

Love from Lambie

When you have finished, colour Lambie in.

Fun in the Sun

Doc and her friends are playing in the sunshine.

Answers on page 68.

Picture Puzzles

Doc is chatting to her friends. How quickly can you answer the questions about this picture?

Colour the heart next to each answer.

1 Where is Doc?

inside ♡

outside ♡

2 How many children are in the picture?

3 ♡

4 ♡

3 What instrument is Donny playing?

guitar ♡

drums ♡

1 Where is Doc?

inside ♡

outside ♡

2 How many cups are on the table?

2 ♡

3 ♡

3 Who is wearing a pink hat?

Doc ♡

Lambie ♡

How well did you do?

What's Wrong?

Help Doc work out what's wrong with teddy by colouring in this picture.

36

Helpful Hallie

Hallie is checking Doc's supplies. Can you count the items and help her decide which pile is bigger?

Tick the pile which has MORE items in it.

1   **a**   **b**

2   **a**   **b**

3   **a**   **b**

37

Answers on page 68.

Gulpy Gators

1

Doc and Donny are playing a game. Each of the hungry alligators must gulp down as many marbles as they can.

2

When Doc goes to get a drink, Donny adds an extra bag of marbles into the game. Now the gators can really get gulping!

3

"Donny, what's wrong?" asks Doc when she comes back. "The game's broken," he says. "One of the gators won't gulp anymore."

"Oh no! I'll take a look at it, Donny, maybe I can fix it."
"Thanks, Doc," says Donny.

4 Doc takes the game to her surgery. The Doc is in! "Hi, everyone!" calls Doc to her toys.

5 "We have a new patient. These are the gulpy gators although one of them isn't very gulpy."

6

"I'm Gustave. I don't feel very well," says the green gator.
"Don't worry, I'm going to help you," says Doc.

"Stuffy, you're in charge of the rest of the gators while I take Gustave to the check-up room."

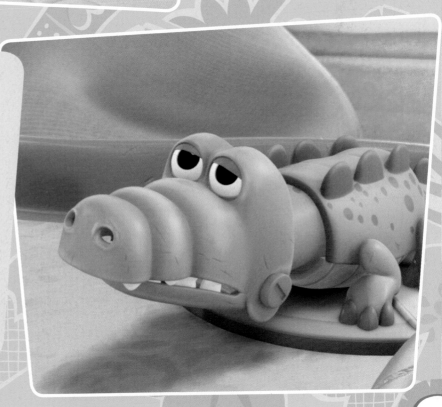

"Sure thing, Doc! Dragons are great at being in cha-aaa-aa-arge!" yelps Stuffy as the gators snap at his tail.

8

"They're gulping up everything!" cries Doc. "I don't feel like eating anything," groans Gustave.

9

"Hmm, that's interesting," says Doc. "I didn't want to eat anything earlier because I was full after my snack."

Doc has a diagnosis. "Gustave, you have Stuffedfulliosis!" she says. "What's that?" Gustave asks.

10 "You've eaten too many marbles and now you're really full. You should stop eating when you feel full," explains Doc.

11 "That makes sense, Donny did give us lots of extra marbles," agrees Gustave. "No wonder you feel ill," says Doc.

12 Doc opens the lid on Gustave's tummy and takes all the marbles out. "Hey, I feel hungry again!" he shouts happily.

13 "Then let's take you back to Donny for another game," says Doc. "Thanks, Doc. I feel marble-ous now!" laughs Gustave.

the end

Look for the Book

Oh no, Doc has lost her Big Book of Boo-Boos!

Which path does she need to follow to find it?

Answers on page 68.

Tracing Trails

Use a pen or pencil to trace each of these lines.

Start at each dot and follow the trail to see who each item belongs to.

Perfect Pairs

Draw lines to match these pictures of Doc and her friends into pairs.

Circle the picture that doesn't have a match.

1

2

3

4

Answers on page 68.

Lend a Hand

The surgery is busy today. Can you help Doc with her check-ups by completing these activities?

1 Help Doc fill in this chart by tracing over the dotted lines.

2 Make sure Doc has everything she needs by finishing this picture of her bag.

4 What does Doc always wear around her neck? Trace over the dotted lines to find out.

3 Doc doesn't have time to finish this chart. Can you fill in the rest of it for her?

Answers on page 68.

Odd One Out

Look carefully at the pictures below.
Can you spot the odd one out in each row?

1

a   b   c   d

2

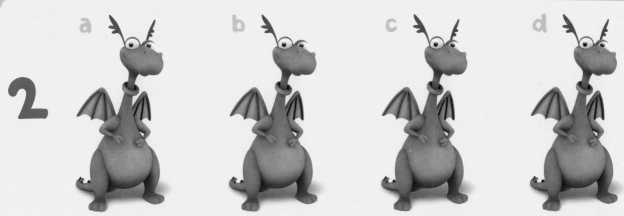

a   b   c   d

3

a   b   c   d

Answers on page 68.

Doc's Surgery

Doc is examining a patient. Can you spot the close-ups below in the big picture?

a

Tick ✔ a circle as you spot each close-up.

How many friends are watching Doc's examination?
Trace over the correct number.

1 or 2

Another patient needs Doc. Can you spot the close-ups below in the big picture?

Tick ✔ a circle as you spot each close-up.

How many friends are watching this examination? Trace over the correct number.

 or

49

Answers on page 68.

Knight Time

Can Doc find a cure for an icky sticky knight? Read this funny story to find out …

Doc and her toys are playing a make-believe game of Princesses and Knights. Princess Lambie is trapped in a castle tower. If only there were a brave knight who could rescue her!

"Here I come," yells Stuffy. "A brave knight to the rescue-ooo-ouch!" Stuffy slips and lands with a thump. Lambie isn't very impressed!

"Doc, can't a real knight in shining armour rescue me for once?" she asks. "Donny used to have a toy knight, perhaps he can play our game," says Doc. "But what about me?" asks Stuffy. "You're the scary dragon," Doc replies. "I'd be great at that! Rarrrr!" roars Stuffy.

Doc asks Donny if she can borrow his knight. She finds him hidden under Donny's bed. Doc uses her magic stethoscope to bring him to life.

"Wow, a real knight in shining armour!" says Lambie. "I am Sir Kirby, the bravest knight of them all! How may I serve you, Princess Lambie?" he asks. "I need rescuing from this scary dragon," says Lambie.

"Do not fear, I shall save yooooouuu ... oops!" Lambie gasps as the knight falls over. "Sir Kirby? Are you OK?" asks Hallie. "It seems my legs aren't working very well. Or my arms!" says Sir Kirby. "Even my suit of armour doesn't shine anymore. I'm a hopeless knight," he sighs.

"Sir Kirby, I think you need a check-up," says Doc, as she goes to pick him up. "Oh! You seem to be all sticky!" "I do?" he asks. "What's wrong with me?" Doc doesn't know. "But I promise I'll work it out," she tells the knight. "The Doc is in!"

"What are those shiny things?" Sir Kirby asks nervously, looking at Doc's doctor's bag. "Don't worry, these are the tools I use to help my patients feel better," Doc replies. "I'm checking your heart ... sounds good. Now stand against this wall so that I can measure you. Your height is good, you can step away now." But Sir Kirby can't move! "I appear to be stuck!" he cries.

Stuffy helps to unstick Sir Kirby from the wall. Doc examines his armour with her magnifying glass. "Ew, it looks like you're covered in sticky jam and pizza cheese! When was the last time you had a bath?" she asks. "A bath? I've never had a bath!" replies the knight.

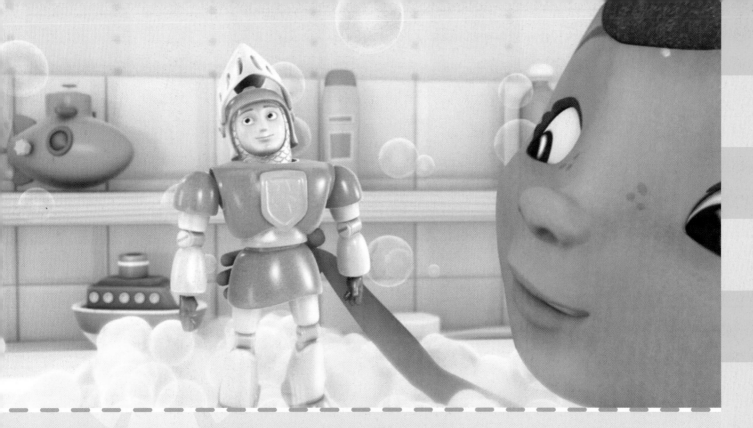

"Sir Kirby, I have a diagnosis," says Doc. "You have Filthy-Icky-Sticky Disease!" Sir Kirby looks shocked. "But is there a cure?" he asks. "You're covered in sticky food, that's why you're sticking to everything. A bath will cure you!" laughs Doc.

Doc's mum runs a bubble bath and Doc washes all the ickiness off Sir Kirby. Soon he's as good as new! "I feel so much better. Now I can rescue Princess Lambie!" he cries. "Ah, my knight in shiny armour!" says Lambie and everybody laughs.

the end

Favourite Friends

Doc is hanging out with her family and toy friends. Help her complete the activity below.

Can you match each shadow to its owner? The first one has been done for you.

Doc   Dad   Stuffy   Hallie   Lambie

Well done!

Mum Chilly Donny Squeakers

Answers on page 68.

On the Go

Doc's friends are hitching a ride! Add some bright colours to this fun picture.

Who is it?

Doc has been taking photos of her friends.
Can you work out who is in each picture?

a

L _ _ _ _ _ _

b

Write the
name of each friend
underneath the
pictures.

The first letters
have been added to
help you.

C _ _ _ _

H _ _ _ _ _

S _ _ _ _ _

Say CHEESE!

Answers on page 68.

Puzzle Time

Join Doc and her friends in the clinic to solve these tricky teasers.

Hallie in a Hurry

Hallie has been rushing around the clinic helping Doc. Follow the trail she's made with your finger or a pencil.

What's Missing?

Chilly is missing something in each of these pictures. Can you work out what?

a

b

c

Lambie's Letters

Lambie needs your help to solve this puzzle.
Look at the objects below then colour the
letter that each one begins with.

 1

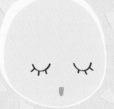 **a** **s** **o**

2

 **b** **r** **m**

3

 **p** **e** **f**

Answers on page 68.

Stuffy's Check-up

Use the little image below to help you colour this picture of Doc listening to Stuffy's chest.

Size Sorter

Find your favourite pen then answer the questions below by circling the correct pictures.

1 Which picture of Doc is the smallest?

a  b  c

2 Which picture of Hallie is the biggest?

a  b  c

3 Which two pictures of Stuffy are the same size?

a  b  c

Answers on page 68.

Arcade Escapade

1

Doc's family are at the amusement arcade. Doc and Donny can't wait to play their favourite games!

2

Doc rushes to the race car game. "Lambie, you can help me steer!" she giggles as she presses the start button.

3

Suddenly Doc hears a noise. "Did somebody just call my name?" she asks.

Doc looks around. "The toys in the toy grabber tank are calling me!" she says, heading towards the game.

"We've heard that you can fix toys," says a pink bear. "My friend, Gaby the Giraffe, really needs your help."

"A little girl tried to win me but the grabber tore my leg," says Gaby. "Now nobody wants to me because I'm broken."

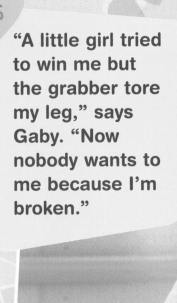

"I'll do everything I can to fix you," says Doc. "But first I need to play the game to get you out of this tank."

8

"It's very difficult," says the pink bear. "But we have to help Gaby," says Doc as she presses the start button. "Here we go!"

9

"To the left, right a bit ... there!" says Doc. The grabber picks up Gaby and starts to lift but ... oh no! It drops her.

10

"This job needs a dragon!" yells Stuffy. "I'll climb in and hold onto Gaby as the grabber pulls me out." "That's so brave," says Doc.

Stuffy climbs into the tank and holds Gaby. Doc lifts them out. They've done it! Now Doc must mend Gaby's leg.

12

Doc pushes the stuffing in and ties the thread. "All better!" she says. "Thanks, Doc. Perhaps I'll find a new home now," says Gaby.

13

"Why don't you come home with us?" suggests Doc. "That would be lovely," cries Gaby and everyone cheers.

Gaby waves goodbye to her friends in the tank. "We'll come back and visit you soon," says Doc.

the end

Answers

Page 8 Say Hello
1 – Stuffy, 2 – Chilly, 3 – Doc,
4 – Lambie, 5 – Hallie.

Page 10 Let's Explore

Page 16 Bath Time
Bath Buddies: 1 – c, 2 – a, 3 – b.
Time for the Tub: 1 – d, 2 – a,
3 – c, 4 – b.

Page 17 Daring Differences

Page 19 Pet Vet
There are 6 dog bowls.

Pages 20-21 Colour Fun
Doctor's Kit: Doc's bag
is pink.
Riding Around: Doc's hair band,
Doc's top, Doc's stethoscope,
Doc's socks and Hallie
are purple.

Page 22 Cuddle Time
Piece b finishes the picture.

Pages 28-29 The Doc is In!
Counting Fun: There are
10 plasters.
Little Lambie: Picture c is
the smallest.
Time to Play!: Doc has
bought a ball. The friends
will play catch.

Page 30 The Letter d
Dice, dog, duck and domino.

Pages 32-33 Fun in the Sun
6 balls, 4 sunglasses and 5
flowers.

Pages 34-35 Picture Puzzles
Puzzle 1: 1 – outside, 2 – 3,
3 – drums.
Puzzle 2: 1 – inside, 2 – 3,
3 – Lambie.

Page 37 Helpful Hallie
1 – a, 2 – b, 3 – a.

Page 42 Look for the Book
Doc needs to take path c.

Pages 44-45 Perfect Pairs
1 and 4, 2 and 3, 5 and 9, 7 and 8.
6 doesn't have a match.

Page 46 Lend a Hand
4 - a stethoscope.

Page 47 Odd One Out
1 – c, 2 – b, 3 – a.

Pages 48-49 Doc's Surgery
a – 2 friends are watching,
b – 3 friends are watching.

Pages 54-55 Favourite Friends

Pages 58-59 Who is it?
a – Lambie, b – Chilly,
c – Hallie, d – Stuffy.

Pages 60-61 Puzzle Time
What's Missing?: a – hat,
b – button, c – nose.
Lambie's Letters: 1 – s for sun,
2 – b for ball, 3 – f for flower.

Page 63 Size Sorter
1 – b, 2 – c, 3 – a and b.

Have you seen our other Annuals?

Entertaining **stories**

Puzzles and **Games**

Colouring Pages

Available NOW!